In a flash the horse's eyes were wild. His nostrils flared. He blew through his nose and leaped to the farthest corner of the pen. In spite of everything, the fire in the horse's body made him a breathtaking sight.

At that moment Garnet knew she must find a way to free the proud Arabian from his filthy stall.

The Wild Arabian

by Marilyn D. Anderson
illustrations by Bill Robison

Published by Willowisp Press
801 94th Avenue North, St. Petersburg, Florida 33702

Printed in the United States of America
2 4 6 8 10 9 7 5 3

ISBN 0-87406-207-1

For my husband, Ken

One

IT was a terrible dream. An evil power had her at its mercy. Part of her wanted to wake up. Another part of her hurt so badly that she wanted to stay asleep.

As Garnet Grant became conscious, she saw a huge piece of white cement lying on the bed. She remembered an accident. That piece of cement was her leg!

"Mom," she moaned. "Mom, where am I?"

"Garnet darling, thank heaven," came her mother's voice from somewhere very close. Then Mrs. Grant's face was smiling down at her.

"What happened?" Garnet demanded. "What did they do to me?"

"Shhh," said her mom soothingly. "You have a

broken leg. You wouldn't let them set it. The doctor gave you some medicine to make you sleep. In about six weeks you'll be good as new."

"It hurts, Mom," Garnet whimpered.

Mrs. Grant put her arm around her daughter. "I know, honey. That's why they want to keep you here overnight. They also want to be sure that bump on your head didn't do any real damage."

"Oh," answered Garnet more softly. "What happened to me? I was riding Dandy, and I remember falling."

"Your horse probably stepped in a hole or just tripped," Garnet's older sister, Jeannie, said. "You should have known better than to go riding with no one home."

"She's right," Mrs. Grant agreed. "We're lucky Mrs. Prentice saw you fall. If she hadn't been looking out her window at just the right time, you might have lain there for hours."

"Is Dandy all right?" Garnet asked suddenly.

"He's fine. He's not even lame," Jeannie informed her. "Of course, you'll probably be afraid of horses from now on."

"Jeannie!" her mother said sharply.

"Well, they always say you will be if you don't get right back on," Jeannie explained.

"That is ridiculous," Mrs. Grant said angrily. "Garnet couldn't possibly have gotten back on, and the horse did not throw her."

"I'll be riding again real soon," Garnet promised. "I miss Dandy already."

"You sure can't ride with that plaster cast on your leg," Jeannie said.

Garnet realized that her sister was probably right. Oh, well, she thought, at least the cast would be off before school was out. There would still be time for her to get Dandy ready for the county fair.

When she got home the next day, Garnet insisted on hobbling out to see her horse. She wanted to make sure he knew that she didn't blame him for what had happened.

It was several days before she could manage well enough to at least brush Dandy. Riding was definitely out. Getting around school was going to be enough of a challenge.

Garnet envied Jeannie for the fine condition her sister's horse, Princess, was already in. The palomino mare had been kept in and blanketed for weeks so that her skin was silky smooth. Also, Jeannie rode Princess faithfully on any day the weather allowed. Garnet knew that her sister had a good chance of winning the top trophy at the fair this year. That trophy was for the overall best 4-H horseman or horsewoman in the county.

On one Saturday morning Garnet was hobbling around trying to clean Dandy's stall when Jeannie and a friend came into the barn. The friend was a good-looking boy that Garnet had never seen before. It was embarrassing for her to be caught in her most ragged jeans doing such a dirty job. She wondered if Jeannie had done it on purpose.

Looking perfect as usual, Jeannie explained, "This is my family's stable." She acted surprised to see Garnet, and added, "Believe it or not, this

is my little sister."

The boy offered his hand. "Glad to meet you. I'm Scott Morgan."

Garnet rubbed her hand on her dirty jeans before taking his. She couldn't think of a thing to say. Of course, that didn't matter because Jeannie was talking again.

"Scott just moved in on the other side of town. He's going to ride his bike over often so that I can teach him all about horses," Jeannie announced.

Garnet knew why her sister was being so helpful. Jeannie liked boys. They moved closer to Dandy as Jeannie continued talking.

"That's Garnet's gelding, Dandy. She used to ride him almost every day before her accident. She hasn't ridden him since."

Garnet was furious. That's a dumb thing to say, she wanted to protest. It's obvious why I haven't ridden. Just wait until I get this stupid cast off, she thought.

As if he'd read her mind, Scott said, "I don't

see how she could ride with that cast. Was it the horse's fault?"

"No, silly," Jeannie chirped, putting her hand on Scott's shoulder in a cozy way. "Dandy is a very gentle horse."

Then Jeannie said proudly, "This is my horse, Princess. Isn't she gorgeous?"

Right on cue, Scott responded, "She's just the right horse for you . . . a blond, too."

They were still having a sickeningly sweet conversation when Garnet left. "How dumb," she fumed.

A few days later, Scott asked Garnet if he could ride Dandy. She had to agree because the horse did need exercise.

Jeannie was all cutesy about helping Scott put the saddle on the horse. Garnet couldn't stand to watch her sister so she left. Later when Garnet asked how Scott had done, Jeannie just said, "FINE," and batted her eyes.

Six weeks later Garnet's cast finally came off. She couldn't wait to get home to ride Dandy. When she arrived at the stables she found Scott already riding him. Dandy had given Scott a lot of rides in the last few weeks. But this time no one had asked for her permission. Well, it's my turn to ride, she thought. Scott and Jeannie can think of something else to do.

Garnet walked toward them determinedly. Jeannie pretended not to see her. However, Scott came right over.

"Hi, there," he greeted. "I see you're ready to ride your own horse. I'm glad your cast is off."

Is it looking in Scott's eyes at such close range that makes me stammer foolishly? she wondered. Or was it the thought of riding again? "Yes, ah, er, ah . . . ," she babbled.

Scott swung down off the horse and handed Garnet the reins. Suddenly she felt too weak to get on by herself. "Will you hold Dandy still for me?" she heard herself asking.

Scott looked surprised. But he said with a

shrug, "Guess you're a little out of practice."

Jeannie rode up. "So you're really going to ride again," she said doubtfully.

Garnet hesitated. She turned the stirrup and raised her left foot. The stirrup slipped out of her grasp. She managed to grab it again.

Jeannie looked smugly at her. Scott looked uncomfortable.

This time Garnet forced herself to hold on to the stirrup. She swung up on the horse clumsily. At once panic hit her. Her knees were watery. Dandy shifted his weight, and her heart pounded. She couldn't breathe.

"Are you ready yet?" Scott asked.

"What?" Garnet gasped.

"I mean, should I let go?" he asked a little louder.

Garnet's body seemed frozen. Her face was pale. "No," she almost shrieked. "No, I don't want to ride after all."

With that she slid off the horse and fled. Hot tears stung her cheeks.

☆ ☆ ☆ ☆ ☆

Garnet was in her bedroom, hiding behind a book when Jeannie came in.

"You really are afraid, aren't you?" Jeannie challenged.

"Afraid?" Garnet protested weakly. "What do you mean?"

"You know what I mean," Jeannie insisted. "I figured you would be. Too bad. Well, Scott will be happy to ride Dandy for you."

Just then Mrs. Grant walked in with a load of groceries. "Will one of you please get the other bags?" she asked.

Garnet was relieved when Jeannie went off to help.

Two

ONLY cowards are afraid of horses, Garnet thought unhappily. I guess that means I'm a coward.

She stopped going to the barn. She couldn't face Dandy any more. Scott came over often. Several times he asked her if she minded him riding Dandy. What could she say? A horse should be ridden.

The school was out at last. Still Garnet avoided the barn.

One night Mrs. Grant called a family council meeting. When they were all seated, she began firmly, "You both know that we have been a little short on money since your father left. Now it seems that we own a valuable horse that is only used by the neighbors. Garnet, you don't even go to the barn anymore. Jeannie tells me she does all your chores."

Mrs. Grant waited to see if Garnet had anything to say. Then she continued, "Scott's father has offered us a thousand dollars for Dandy. I need to know if you are going to ride again, Garnet. If not, I will sell the horse."

Garnet was scared. Her mother sounded serious. "Mom, don't sell him," she wailed. "He's part of the family. I'll ride again. You'll see."

Mrs. Grant looked skeptical, but she nodded. "Okay, Mr. Morgan would like an answer by the end of the week. If you have ridden Dandy by then, we'll keep him," she said.

Garnet was at the barn every day that week. She realized how much she missed her horse. She brushed and curried Dandy. She rubbed her hands all over him. Maybe the contact with his body would give her courage, she hoped. But it didn't.

There were two days left until the deadline

when Garnet went for a ride in the country with her mother. Mrs. Grant sold cosmetics to earn some spare dollars. Frequently, she called on people she didn't know.

This particular day they inched their way down a long, muddy driveway. Two sagging buildings greeted them at the driveway's end. A tattered curtain fluttered through a broken window of the larger building. The smaller building looked unused.

"I think I'm wasting my time here," said Mrs. Grant, putting the car into reverse.

Suddenly a huge man with a bushy mustache appeared at the side of the car. He wore ragged jeans and muddy boots.

"What can I do for you?" his deep voice challenged.

"I'm selling beauty aids," said Mrs. Grant in her most charming tone. "Does anyone here use cosmetics?"

Garnet didn't hear the answer. Her attention was suddenly fixed on a movement inside the smaller building. Then a horse's head poked out. It's huge eyes were almost covered by a tangled mass of hair. Those eyes, from what Garnet could see, looked terribly sad.

"What kind of a horse is that?" Garnet interrupted.

The man's beady eyes glittered. "Do you want to see?"

Mrs. Grant shot Garnet a warning look, but Garnet was halfway out of the car and on her way to the shed. Mrs. Grant waited in the car.

The shed was damp and dimly lit. At first all Garnet could see was the outline of the horse. It appeared to be quite tall behind the makeshift fence. Then she realized the horse stood on many layers of dirty straw. Actually the horse was small and appeared to be young. It was impossible to tell what color he was under the filth that covered him.

"This is a purebred Arabian gelding," the man said proudly. "His grandpa was a national champion."

"How old is he? Where did he come from?" Garnet wondered.

"He's two. Got him at a sale last fall."

"Why did you buy him?" she had to ask. Surely this huge man wouldn't ride such a small horse.

"That's a good question," the man grunted. "He did look pretty, and Arabians used to be worth lots of money. Now I don't know what to do with him."

Garnet was looking at the horse's sad eyes again. "Is he for sale?" she asked.

"You bet," the man said hungrily. "I'd take $400."

Garnet remembered at once that she couldn't buy a horse. She knew she ought to be getting back to the car. "Gee, $400 is a lot of money," she said.

"How about $300?" the man answered quickly.

"I don't have $300 either," she admitted. Garnet turned to go. But she had to have one last look. "Is he gentle?"

"He leads all right," the man said hopefully.

"Think your dad might buy him for you?"

"Dad doesn't live with us anymore," she answered softly. "And Mom can hardly afford the horses we do have. Can I pet him anyway?"

The big man nodded. Garnet reached her hand slowly toward the horse. In a flash the horse's eyes were wild. His nostrils flared. He blew through his nose and leaped to the farthest corner of the pen. In spite of everything, the fire in the horse's body made him a breathtaking sight.

At that moment Garnet knew she must find a way to free the proud Arabian from his filthy stall.

Finally the man said, "Well, if you change your mind, my name is George Smith. Tell your mom I'd take $250."

Garnet's mom didn't say anything as they headed out the driveway. After they had driven a few miles, Garnet couldn't stand it any longer. "You should have seen the beautiful horse shut up in that awful building, Mom. I wish someone nice would buy him," she hinted.

"Well, maybe someone who needs another horse will," Mrs. Grant answered firmly.

☆   ☆   ☆   ☆   ☆

Garnet thought about nothing but the Arabian the whole next day. The memory of the horse's sad eyes haunted her. She didn't dare talk about buying him. Everyone knew she didn't ride the horse she had.

Garnet had actually forgotten about the deadline on Dandy. But her mother brought it up that afternoon. Suddenly, Garnet realized there might be a way to save the Arabian.

"You've had one week to prove that you want to ride Dandy again," Mrs. Grant said. She sounded disappointed. "Because you haven't done it, I've decided to sell Dandy next Saturday."

"Mom," Garnet answered eagerly, "I've decided we should sell him. Only I want part of the money to spend."

Mrs. Grant took the announcement by surprise. "Why Garnet, I thought you loved that horse!" she said.

Jeannie was pleased. "Scott will appreciate Dandy a lot more than you do," she said, smiling.

"I need the money to buy something special," Garnet explained.

"What?" her mother demanded.

"It's a secret so far," said Garnet.

"Hmmm," said Mrs. Grant. "I can't imagine what you might want more than Dandy."

"It's something very important," Garnet pleaded.

"And how much will it cost?" her mother asked.

"Two hundred and fifty dollars," Garnet said, trying to stay calm.

"We can't afford to waste $250, Garnet," her mother answered firmly.

"I know, Mom," Garnet assured her. "This is something that will gain in value."

"I hope you know what you're doing," said her

mother doubtfully.

Garnet continued earnestly. "Oh, Mom, I know it's a lot of money. But look, you'll have $750. Please, Mom, it's awfully important."

"All right," Mrs. Grant sighed at last. "You may have the $250. I just hope we can take back whatever it is if you've made a mistake."

"Thank you!" Garnet exploded.

Three

IT was the next day before Garnet could make her important call in private. Carefully she dialed Mr. Smith's number. She waited nervously for him to answer.

"Hello," said a gruff voice.

"Hello, Mr. Smith?" Garnet said, trying to sound older. "Do you still have your Arabian?"

The man's voice then became friendly. "The Arabian? Yes, yes, I still have him."

"Well, I want to buy him. Can you deliver him on Saturday?" Garnet asked.

There was complete silence on the other end of the phone. Then Mr. Smith asked suspiciously, "Is this a joke? You sound like a kid."

"I *am* a kid," Garnet admitted. "I came with

the cosmetics lady two days ago. My mom said I could have your horse."

Mr. Smith thought for a moment. Then he said, "All right. Where do I deliver him?"

Garnet wanted to yell for joy. Instead she gave the man directions. She asked him to come about 11 A.M. Scott and his dad should have picked up Dandy by then.

Nothing worked out Saturday as planned. Scott's dad had a flat tire on the rental trailer. They didn't even arrive until after 10 o'clock. Then Dandy didn't want to get in. It was almost 11 o'clock before the endgate closed behind the horse. Seeing Dandy ready to leave made Garnet want to cry. She wished she could cancel the whole deal.

Just then a noisy truck pulled into the driveway. Garnet realized with a sinking feeling that the Arabian had arrived. Horrors! Jeannie

28

would make nasty remarks about him. Scott and his father would think she was crazy to buy such an animal. Her mother might not let her keep him.

The huge man came toward them in his filthy jeans. Garnet noticed that even his shoe laces were a mess.

"Morning, folks." Smith greeted them importantly. "I'm here to deliver a horse. Just give me my check, and I'll be on my way."

Garnet's mom was speechless. "There must be some mistake," she said at last. "We're selling a horse, not buying one."

"I believe your daughter bought his one," the man said warily. "She said she had your permission."

"My daughter?" asked Mrs. Grant, puzzled. Suddenly she made the connection. "Garnet, it was that horse you wanted to buy. I might have known."

No one said a word. Then Mrs. Grant gave a big sigh. "All right, let's see it," she decided.

Everyone wanted to see the horse at once. They hurried to the back of the truck and looked in. Four jaws dropped at the sight of the skinny, dirty creature they saw cowering in the truck's corner.

"What a mess!" Jeannie announced in disgust. "I can't believe she did this!"

Mr. Smith looked worried. "He's kind of dirty, but he's a purebred Arabian," he grumbled.

"Can you prove it? Does he have any papers?" Jeannie shot back.

"Yes, ma'am," the man answered angrily.

Just then Garnet came to Mr. Smith's rescue. "I only want this horse for a pet," she pleaded. "Will you stop picking on him?"

Everyone was quiet while Mrs. Grant thought. "I guess I did make a promise to Garnet," she said at last. "Was it $250 you wanted, Mr. Smith?"

Smith nodded.

"All right," Mrs. Grant agreed. "Please unload the horse. I will write the check."

Eagerly the man took the check and gave Mrs. Grant the horse's papers. He hauled the horse around like a toy and shoved the animal out in a heap. Minutes later he was gone.

The frightened little horse landed on his knees. Quickly he struggled to his feet. His body filled with wildfire. His dark eyes haunted Garnet. Suddenly Garnet made a wild grab for the halter rope. Luckily Scott grabbed hold too or she never could have stopped the horse.

"Garnet, he's wild," Scott whispered. "What are you going to do with him?"

"Make him happy," she muttered.

"Let's get him to the barn before he escapes," Mr. Morgan suggested.

The Arabian was very upset. He struggled so hard that it took everyone's help to get him to the barn.

"Good luck, Garnet," said Scott when he regained his breath.

"You have a real project there," added Mr. Morgan as they turned to go.

"Wait a minute," called Jeannie. "I'll go with you to help."

Garnet and her mother stared at the new horse for a few minutes. Finally Mrs. Grant said with a sigh, "I hope this works out for the best. That horse certainly does need help." Then she walked to the house.

The terror in the horse's eyes was almost gone now. The look he gave Garnet was full of questions.

Garnet leaned on the stall door and said soothingly, "You poor little guy. I didn't realize you were so thin. From now on there will be plenty to eat and a dry bed. I promise."

After Garnet changed her clothes, she brought some feed. The horse moved farther back in the stall as she put the feed in his box. When she moved away, he continued to watch her.

At last the horse inched forward to sniff at the feed. He stared at Garnet again. She was still. Cautiously, he took a mouthful and stepped back in the corner to chew it. He continued to watch Garnet between mouthfuls. Gradually he spent more time eating and less time watching.

When the feed was gone, Garnet brought a flake of hay to the stall. Again the huge eyes studied her. At last the horse came forward to sniff her hair. She stood absolutely still. He sniffed her shoulders and her hands. Then he began to eat the hay.

Later Garnet brought a brush. The horse moved to the farthest possible corner. She entered the stall and gently touched him with her hand. She could feel him tremble. When he relaxed a little, she brushed his back lightly. She found that under the dirt was a black horse with scattered white hairs.

You'll be a beautiful gray horse someday, she thought.

Just then, Jeannie burst into the barn. The Arabian almost knocked Garnet to the floor in his hurry to get away.

"You scared him," Garnet scolded her.

"That horse is afraid of his shadow," Jeannie

countered. "Boy, is he dirty. I hope he doesn't give Princess lice."

"He doesn't have lice," Garnet said angrily. At least she hoped he didn't.

"Does he have a name?" Jeannie asked.

"I don't know," Garnet realized. "I forgot to look at his papers."

"I'd just call him 'Loser.' " Jeannie laughed.

"Never mind. I didn't ask for your opinion," Garnet exploded.

Later Garnet asked her mother for the papers. She found that her horse did have a name. It was "Sasha's Sparkler." Sasha was his mother's name.

"Sparkler," Garnet said aloud. "That fits him. Or it will when I've had him for a while."

Four

THE next day was Sunday. Garnet got up very early to spend some time with Sparkler before going to church. She just *had* to get him cleaned up today.

She gave Sparkler and Jeannie's horse some feed. For a moment she stood, enjoying the sight of her horse eating. She felt warm all over to have given him this clean, airy stall.

When Sparkler was finished eating, Garnet attacked the snarls in his mane. He did not seem to appreciate her efforts. She finally had to tie him to make him stand still.

Grooming his body was really a project, Garnet found out. Manure and straw had dried as hard as cement. The awful stuff covered the whole bottom half of Sparkler's body. It looked terrible. She couldn't get either the brush or the curry comb to move through it. She tried pulling off hunks with her fingers. But large patches of hair came with the hunks.

Garnet wondered if soap and water would help. She took the horse in the aisle and held the reins. He rolled his eyes at the bucket of suds. He leaped into the air when she touched him with a wet rag. She tried again and again until he began to kick at her.

Now Garnet was angry. Sparkler isn't very grateful for my kindness, she thought. Then she had an idea. She filled a spray bottle with the suds. Now, with it she could squirt at him from safety. Soon the horse realized that it did no good to fight. He settled down and took his bath like a gentleman.

When he was all wet, Garnet tried the curry comb again. It still didn't work very well. She found the only way to loosen the hard stuff was with her bare hands. It wasn't long before her

clothes, as well as both arms, were covered with green filth.

Suddenly Jeannie was at the door. She was all dressed up.

"Yuck! What are you doing?" Jeannie squealed. "You're a mess. The barn is a mess. Don't you know it's time to go to church?"

Garnet looked down at her green slimy clothes. She gave Jeannie a sickly smile. "Gosh, I forgot the time. How long do I have to get ready?"

"About five minutes," Jeannie told her, walking away. Then she yelled back, "And I'm not sitting by you."

Garnet put Sparkler back in his stall, soap suds and all. She rinsed her arms under the faucet and ran into the house.

Later that afternoon Garnet brought Sparkler out into the aisle to wash him down. He really looked awful now with the half-melted hunks hanging all over him. At least he behaved this time, she thought. After awhile he began to look better. Unfortunately, the barn began to look worse.

The sunlight streaming in the barn window made Garnet decide to take the horse outside to dry. She knew he'd be hard to control. What she needed was a chain to put over his nose. The only thing she could find was Jeannie's new show halter. She decided to use it.

The second they were outside, the Arabian charged forward. Garnet was pulled along behind until she managed to plant her feet. Then she hauled on the chain. Sparkler whirled toward her in surprise. After a few more pulls on the chain, he was following her nicely.

Garnet was feeling pretty good about Sparkler when they started back toward the barn. They were just coming through the door when a barn cat ran under Sparkler. He leaped wildly to the side. There was a ripping noise as the halter caught on something sharp. Suddenly the horse was loose in the barn.

Quickly Garnet shut the barn door. She opened his stall door and got some feed. She was relieved when Sparkler finally went in his stall after it.

"It's time I look over the damage," Garnet said to herself. Grooming tools were scattered. There was a broken liniment bottle to clean up. The wet goo had been kicked all around. Hay was everywhere. Jeannie's show halter was ruined.

Garnet sighed. She didn't know where to begin. She'd have to tell Jeannie about the halter right away. But she'd be in a lot of trouble if anyone saw the barn looking this way.

Then, before she could get started, the worst possible thing happened. Jeannie came in. She was dressed for riding. Jeannie stopped and stared. Then she screamed, "What happened here? This place looks like a cyclone hit it!"

Garnet started to open her mouth to explain. But Jeannie saw the halter before Garnet had a chance.

"Is that my new show halter?" Jeannie screeched in a terrible voice. "It is!" she said, grabbing it. "You've ruined it! You, you idiot!"

"I'm sorry. Really I am," Garnet mumbled.

"You're going to be a lot sorrier when Mom hears about this," Jeannie threatened. With that, she turned and stalked off toward the house.

Garnet knew she was in trouble now.

By the next afternoon Garnet had forgiven Sparkler for making her lose all of her allowance for the next month. "It really wasn't your fault," she told him.

They stood looking out the window. Garnet decided today was a good time to let the horse outside. The fenced-in area that adjoins the barn seems like a safe place for him, she thought.

Garnet used the chain from Jeannie's broken halter to lead the horse to the pen. Since I'm paying for it, I might as well use it, she thought. Once outside, Garnet undid the chain, but she left the halter on.

Sparkler walked a few steps and looked around. He didn't seem to know he was free. Then, with a wild buck and a huge bound, he crossed the little pen. He almost ran into the fence before he stopped. He began to circle the pen at a prancing trot. Soon he was laying in the grass having a good roll. Then there was more bucking, running, and trotting.

When Sparkler settled down to pick at the grass, Garnet decided to leave him alone for a while. She needed to take care of some chores in the house.

A short time later, she thought she heard a dog barking. She ran to the window to see a huge German Shepherd racing around Sparkler's pen. The dog was barking madly.

Inside the pen, Sparkler was getting more and more excited. Before Garnet could get to him, he made a desperate leap over the fence. He didn't quite clear it, though, and the top rail broke under his weight.

Garnet yelled at the dog and waved a broom at him. She recognized the dog as her neighbor's usually harmless pet. The dog seemed very surprised at her attitude and left with his tail between his legs.

Luckily Sparkler had chosen to jump the fence that led to the pasture. It would have been more serious if he had headed for the road.

Garnet ran into the barn for a bucket of grain and a lead rope. She forced herself to walk slowly toward the frightened horse. He stopped snorting and running to look at her. She shook the grain and talked calmly.

"Easy, boy. It's all right," she told him. "That big, mean dog is not going to get you. Come get some grain."

Sparkler never moved a muscle as Garnet snapped on the lead rope. She breathed a sigh of relief and led him back to the barn.

He was very hot so Garnet got a towel and rubbed him down. More of the dried manure came off as she rubbed. She was just thinking how much better he was looking when she noticed a strange bare spot just over his tail. She looked more carefully. The hair looked thin all around it. The skin was scaly.

"Oh, no," she groaned. "What next? I think you really do have lice. Jeannie is going to kill me when she finds out."

For the first time since Sparkler had arrived, Garnet wondered if she should have bought him. Nothing had gone right. She leaned her head against the wall and cried.

A few minutes later she felt a nibbling at her neck. She looked around and was face to face with two huge sad eyes. She just stared into those eyes for several minutes.

Finally, Garnet smiled. "You're worth it," she decided.

Five

DOC Holmes had been the Grants' veterinarian for years. He loved to talk, and he never hurried.

"Hi, Doc," Garnet greeted him warmly.

"Hi yourself, Rocky," Doc answered. He knew "Garnet" was both her name and her birthstone. That made him decide to call her Rocky.

"Your mom tells me you have a new animal. She says she's not quite sure what kind yet," he said mischievously.

"Then she must not have seen Sparkler out for a run," Garnet said. "He's all horse."

"Sparkler, is it? Well, let's see the patient," said Doc, shuffling toward the barn.

Soon Doc was taking the horse's temperature, feeling his legs, and checking his teeth in silence.

Only then did he inspect the bald spot he'd been called to treat.

"Hmmm," the vet said. "This doesn't look good."

"What is it?" Garnet asked nervously.

"Well, among other things, I'd say this young fellow has a case of ringworm. It isn't likely to be fatal. Just wash him every day in some strong shampoo I'll leave with you. AND keep him away from your sister's horse. We can't have Princess getting ringworm, too."

"I'll say," Garnet agreed. She waited politely while Doc had a quiet conversation with Sparkler. Suddenly she realized what he had said earlier.

"What do you mean by 'among other things'?" she asked.

"Oh, you caught that did you?" Doc smiled. "Well, your horse just told me that he has lots of worms in his tummy. Says he needs some vitamins, too. Where did you say you got him?"

"I bought him from Mr. Smith over south of town," Garnet answered.

Doc nodded knowingly. "Mr. Smith, eh? It's a good thing for this horse that you bought him. That man doesn't take good care of his animals."

The veterinarian was thoughtful. "You know, I treated this horse for pneumonia last winter. We almost lost him, too."

"Really?"

"Yup." Doc pulled out his pipe. "I remember this horse well. No matter how sick he was last winter, I always knew he planned to live." The vet sucked at his pipe. "I don't think Smith ever let the horse out. That dampness is what got him sick, I'd bet."

Garnet was shocked. "The whole winter in that awful shed with no exercise? No wonder Sparkler fought so hard when we took him toward our barn."

"That could be it," Doc agreed. "Say, do you want me to go ahead and worm him while I'm here?"

"Sure," she nodded. "Better give him some vitamins, too."

Doc continued to smoke his pipe with no sign that he'd heard. At last he put away the pipe and got out the equipment needed for tube worming.

Garnet dreaded the struggle and mess ahead. Most horses object strongly to having a tube run up the nose and down to the stomach. But Garnet knew this method was the best way to be sure the medicine actually got to the worms.

Luckily Doc was a master at handling horses. He was so gentle that the job was soon done. Sparkler had barely gotten upset.

Outside, Doc relit his pipe and leaned against his truck. "Garnet," he said seriously, "I want to give you some advice about this horse. Arabians are sensitive. Treat them rough and you'll have nothing but trouble. They grow up slower than most breeds, too. You can start riding Sparkler a little around the yard this year. It will be good to get him used to it before he gets any bigger. Just remember not to push him. You might ruin his legs for good if you get him running and jumping with you too early. I want you to do a good job with him because he is going to be one fine horse."

Garnet's eyes shone. Doc was the first person to say a kind word about Sparkler. "Do you really think he's going to be a good horse?" she asked eagerly.

"I know he will," Doc answered. "There's a fineness and balance about all his parts. He strikes me as being quite intelligent, too. Plus, I know all about his father, Spartacus. That stallion never sired anything but champions."

"Doc, how did you know he was fathered by Spartacus?" Garnet wondered. "I never said anything to you about that."

"No, you didn't," Doc chuckled. "But Mr. Smith did. That man went on and on about how valuable his horse was."

Garnet felt happy the rest of the day. She repeated Doc's words to herself several times. "Spartacus never sired anything but champions." Maybe she hadn't been so stupid to buy Sparkler after all.

☆ ☆ ☆ ☆ ☆

Later when Jeannie brought Princess back from a ride, she teased, "Hi, Garnet, how's your loser?"

Garnet just ignored her.

"Planning to ride him soon?" Jeannie asked more pointedly.

"He's not old enough to ride, and you know it," Garnet said angrily.

"Is that so?" Jeannie scoffed. "There are several kids in the 4-H club riding two-year-olds. I don't see why your dumb Arabian is any different."

That did it. Garnet exploded. "For your information, Smarty, Doc Holmes was here today. He said that Sparkler is going to be a very fine horse someday. He also said that Arabians should not be rushed."

"Oh, I don't think you would rush to ride him," Jeannie said smugly. "Just run up lots of bills and never ride the horse. I doubt that Mom will go for that idea long. She'll end up selling this one, too."

Garnet had no answer this time. She wondered if Jeannie was right.

Six

TO Jeannie, summer meant parties, swimming, dating, and the fair. She was pretty and popular. She was always winning something. Mrs. Grant told everyone how proud she was of Jeannie.

Garnet was just glad for more time to be with Sparkler. Her mother tried to get her interested in other activities. But Garnet preferred doing things by herself.

By now Sparkler had lived with the Grants over a month. He had eaten well, taken his vitamins, been wormed, and groomed endlessly. It's beginning to look as if Doc had been right, Garnet thought. Sparkler is a beautiful horse.

Garnet's love had changed the Arabian in other

ways, too. Now he greeted everyone with eager curiosity. He loved being handled. He would stand with eyes half-closed while she brushed every inch of him, including his tail. His once sad eyes shone with happiness.

Every day Garnet taught him new things. He was an eager learner. She took him for walks around the fields. She showed him bicycles, cars, and other noisy things. He got used to dogs. One day she even sat on him while he was lying down.

Mrs. Grant stopped down at the barn one afternoon to take a good look at Sparkler. She seemed surprised. "I do believe he's turning into something special," she said.

Garnet beamed with pride.

"We need to start thinking about his training," Mrs. Grant continued.

Garnet frowned. "Gee, Mom, I *am* training him. He's easy to handle now. He's not afraid of anything."

"That's all very fine, but horses were meant to be ridden," Mrs. Grant said firmly. "He can't just stand around the barn for the rest of his life."

Garnet felt sort of sick. "Why not? He didn't cost very much," she pleaded.

"No, but the bills have been coming in ever since," her mother answered quickly. "There have been feed bills, vet bills, hoof-trimming bills, bills to repair the fence, and Jeannie's broken halter. That horse must be useful."

"Couldn't we wait until next year?" Garnet asked hopefully. "Doc Holmes said Sparkler's legs aren't strong enough yet."

Mrs. Grant shook her head. "I'm sure he's strong enough for a little riding. Breaking him won't be such a big project while he's small. Maybe one of the 4-H boys will work with him."

"But we don't need another riding horse," Garnet tried again.

"Well, if you don't ride him, someone else will," her mother said. "I will not have. an eight hundred-pound pet."

Garnet couldn't stand the thought of someone else riding her horse. The 4-H boys were used to working with quarter horses. They treated horses roughly and would ruin an Arabian. Sparkler would lose all the trust he'd gained in people. She had to stall for time.

"I could get him used to the bridle and saddle," she offered.

"Yes, that would help," Mrs. Grant agreed.

Garnet started that very day. She had read that cowboys start training a horse by "sacking him out." An old blanket ought to do well, she thought. She waved the blanket all around Sparkler. At first his eyes grew big. Soon he was yawning.

Later she put a saddle on his back. She patted Sparkler and told him how brave he was. She cinched the saddle very loosely the first few times. A few days later, she made it snug enough for riding. They took long walks to get him used to the stirrups banging about.

Garnet found the perfect training bit in an old trunk. Dad had probably used it years ago, she thought. It was made of rubber and would be easier on a young horse than metal.

She put the bit gently into Sparkler's mouth and snapped it to his halter rings. He tried to spit it out. When that didn't work, he tried rubbing the ends against the wall. She made him wear it for an hour a day until it was old stuff. Bridling was easy after that.

One day Jeannie saw Garnet putting the bridle and saddle on the horse. "Hey, Sis, what are you up to?" she asked.

"Mom wants him trained so I'm doing it," Garnet said, wrinkling up her nose.

Jeannie was immediately interested. "Oh, yeah? Jeff Pierce breaks horses. You know, the cute guy on the football team? He'd probably like the job."

"Well, don't tell him about it yet," Garnet begged. "So far I'm doing all right."

"Yeah, but you won't ride Sparkler, will you?"

Jeannie challenged. "Someone else will have to do that."

"I don't know if I will or not," Garnet admitted. "This horse has a lot to learn before that anyway."

"Like what?" Jeannie asked doubtfully.

"I'm not exactly sure," Garnet had to admit. "I'm going to get a book on horse training to find out."

"Good luck," Jeannie scoffed.

That same afternoon Garnet went to the public library. She found four different books on horse training. Her 4-H leader gave her something to read, too. All of the books talked about "lunging." She read that having the horse circle on a long line was a good way to teach the horse voice commands. She decided that lunging would be her next step.

Garnet prepared Sparkler for lunging by saddling and bridling him. The books suggested she tie the reins out of the way. One book said that tying them to the stirrups would make the horse keep his head down. That sounds like a good idea, she thought.

The Grants did not own a lunge line. So, Garnet looked around until she found a sturdy cord about fifteen feet long. She fastened this to the side of Sparkler's bit and moved out to the end of the line. When she clucked and waved the switch at him, he ignored her. She clucked again and used the switch lightly. This time he moved forward at once. Soon she had him circling at the walk. She taught him to stop by repeating "whoa" until he stopped. He responded more quickly to her signals on each try.

When they had practiced starting and stopping several times to the left, Garnet circled Sparkler to the right. This direction was more difficult for her. It was hard to handle the switch with her left hand.

Later Garnet patted Sparkler proudly as she unhooked the reins from the stirrups. "What a smart boy you are," she said, praising him.

Since the lunging had been a success, Garnet read some more to find out the next step. Most of

the books suggested driving the horse with long lines to get him used to turning.

After a few more days of work on starting and stopping, Garnet felt Sparkler was ready to begin turning. She saddled and bridled him as before. This time she tied the reins around the saddle horn. She found another long piece of cord so that she could tie one to each side of the bit. She passed the cords through the stirrups so they would not drag the ground. Then she stood about two feet to the left of the horse's left hip. When she clucked he expected to circle. She simply controlled the size of the circle with her long reins. She switched sides often to turn him both ways. He also learned that "whoa" was associated with a pull on the bit.

One afternoon Scott came by the Grant's house looking for Jeannie. He found Garnet.

"Hey, that's pretty neat," he said enthusiastically. "How did you learn to train horses?"

Garnet blushed at his praise. "I just read about it in books. Sparkler's awfully smart."

"Oh, yeah? You must be almost ready to ride him," Scott suggested.

Garnet blushed brighter. "No, I'm not quite ready for that," she said sadly.

"Oh, that's right," Scott remembered. "You haven't ridden since the accident." Then he looked very serious. "You know, you have to start riding again, don't you? That horse loves you. You've got to be the one who rides him."

"But Scott," Garnet protested. "I can't even ride Dandy. How can I ride an unbroken colt?"

"I don't know," he had to admit. "But I think you'll find a way. If you need any help, just ask me."

When Scott left, Garnet wondered if she'd heard him correctly. Handsome Scott Morgan has offered to help me, the nobody, train a horse. Was he just being kind? Would he really help if I asked? she wondered.

Seven

SPARKLER learned quickly. Soon he was quite good at starting, stopping, and turning on the long reins.

Mrs. Grant came out to watch several times. She usually said things like, "That's really good," or "You've taught him a lot."

One day Mrs. Grant said, "I think he's ready to ride. Jeannie says that Jeff Pierce will be able to take Sparkler for training right after the fair."

"But, Mom," Garnet protested. "I don't want him training my horse."

"I know, dear," Mrs. Grant told her. "The fair is two weeks off. By then you'll be used to the idea."

"But Mom . . . ," Garnet began.

"My mind is made up," her mother interrupted. "There are only a few weeks after the fair until school starts again. After that Jeff will be too busy."

Garnet was upset. Jeannie had sure been in a hurry to talk to Jeff, she thought. What a creep! She knew how Garnet felt about the whole deal. Garnet had to think of something quick. She had to prove to her mother that they didn't need Jeff's help.

That afternoon Garnet waited until Jeannie was at the dentist's to dial Scott's number. Would he help her? She doubted it.

"Hello?" said Scott.

"Hello," Garnet answered breathlessly. "Ah . . . Scott, this is Garnet. Will you help me with Sparkler? I want to ride him before the fair."

"Of course. We have a couple of weeks. No problem," Scott assured her. "When should we try it?"

"How about eight o'clock tomorrow morning?" Garnet gasped.

He hesitated. "Gee, I don't know. I might have a ball game. Why so early?"

"Because Mom will be gone, and Jeannie won't be up yet," Garnet confessed.

"Oh, you don't want an audience." Scott laughed. "Well sure, I can probably make it," he said.

"Gee, thanks," said Garnet and she hung up quickly.

Garnet heard Jeannie tiptoe in at 1:15 the next morning. If Jeannie had been out with Scott, then he had stayed out late, too, she thought. He surely wouldn't want to help with Sparkler early in the morning now. What should I do? she wondered. Maybe Scott would help some other day.

By 7 A.M. Garnet had decided. With or without Scott's help, she would ride Sparkler today.

The beautiful gray Arabian came to Garnet the

minute he saw her. He poked her with his nose and begged for attention. She rubbed his shoulders and scratched his back. At last she put him in his stall for feed.

While the horses ate, she paced the floor. Then it was time to saddle up. She put the bridle on over Sparkler's halter and tied him to a fence post behind the barn. She checked the girth. She petted the horse nervously. If she was ever going to get on him, there was no reason to wait any longer.

Garnet put one foot in the stirrup. Sparkler paid no attention. She put some weight on it. Still Sparkler stood quietly. She stepped back to catch her breath. Again she grabbed the stirrup. This time she put all her weight in it. Sparkler looked around curiously. Garnet leaned across his back. He shifted his feet. She lost her courage and slid off.

Just then she heard an angry voice from behind her yell, "Hey, Garnet, why didn't you wait for me?"

Garnet turned around. It was Scott, hurrying her way.

"You could get hurt out here all by yourself," he said.

"Oh, I didn't think you would come," she sputtered.

"I said I would, didn't I?" he answered crossly. "It isn't even eight o'clock yet. Don't you know this is dangerous?"

It sounded like a lecture. Garnet had to admit she deserved one.

When she didn't answer, Scott spoke more gently. "On the way over here I was wondering if you would let me be the first one to sit on your horse."

A wave of gratefulness washed over Garnet. She didn't have to get on Sparkler. Scott would do it for her.

"Oh, would you please?" she begged.

Scott patted Sparkler quietly for a moment. Then he swung up in one easy motion. The horse did not move. But Garnet could see that he was very uncertain. She quickly reassured him and laughed with relief when Sparkler gave a big sigh.

Scott chuckled. "That's how I feel, too," he admitted.

When Scott got off a few minutes later, Garnet stepped back to let him praise the horse. She didn't know what to say. She was so happy. Finally, Sparkler has been mounted for the first time, she thought. He didn't even get frightened. Then she heard Scott say, "Now it's your turn."

"Come on, Garnet," he continued. "Now you have to ride him." Scott moved to hold Sparkler's head and waited.

She knew Scott was right. She must conquer her fear right now. Her knees wouldn't stop shaking as she moved next to the horse. She hoped Sparkler wouldn't sense her fear. She looked nervously at Scott. He gave her an encouraging smile.

Garnet took a deep breath and set her body in motion. Her mind froze. Then she was sitting on Sparkler. For a moment it was awful. She waited for him to explode. All at once she knew he wasn't going to do anything wrong. But he did need her praise. She leaned over and gave the horse a big hug.

"Oh, you darling," she said through tears of joy.

"I didn't know you cared," said Scott mischievously.

Garnet blushed. "You know I meant the horse. But you are pretty special too for helping me."

Scott changed the subject. "Shall I lead him for you?"

"Oh . . . maybe . . . just a few steps," she said uncertainly.

Sparkler followed Scott willingly. Garnet could feel the horse relax as he adjusted to her weight. She almost hated to get off. Still, they must not rush things. Will I be brave enough to do this again? she wondered as she slid off.

She was too happy to speak. She'd mounted Sparkler at last!

Then Scott said it for her, "You did it, Garnet.

Now you won't be afraid any more."

When she was able to speak she said, "Oh, thank you, thank you, Scott. I could never have done it without you."

He seemed quite pleased with himself. "It was pretty exciting. Only I can't understand why you didn't wait for me this morning."

"Well, I figured . . . That is, I knew you and Jeannie . . . I mean, after being out so late last night, I didn't think you'd remember," Garnet finished lamely.

Scott looked puzzled. "What makes you think I was out late? I went to bed early last night. Was Jeannie out late?" he demanded.

Garnet hesitated. Jeannie must have a new boyfriend. Why hadn't she told Scott? she wondered.

"Never mind," said Scott at last. "I can guess the answer. So that's why she's been avoiding me lately."

"I'm sorry," Garnet said. "I hate to give you bad news after what you've just done for me."

"It's not your fault," Scott muttered angrily. "I should have guessed. Well, I have to go now. See you around."

Garnet watched him go. Well, that's the last I'll see of him, she thought sadly. Now he won't want anything to do with the Grants.

Eight

GARNET was in the barn early the next morning. As she saddled Sparkler, she thought about what Scott had said. Maybe I shouldn't try riding the horse without help. But who would help me? she wondered.

Then, surprisingly, Scott walked in. "Hi," he said softly. "Need any help horse-training today?"

Garnet was so happy she wanted to hug him. "You bet," she agreed. "I was afraid you'd hate all us Grants after yesterday."

Scott thought a minute. "Guess I did sort of feel that way at first. I'd really been counting on Jeannie to help me get Dandy ready for the fair."

"Get Dandy ready for the fair?" Garnet echoed.

"Is that what you two were up to?"

Scott looked embarrassed. "Well, maybe there was a little more to it than that," he admitted. "But now it doesn't matter. I don't have a chance trying to compete against all you experienced riders on my own."

Garnet made a face. "You won't be competing with this kid," she reminded him. "Sparkler isn't even ready to show yet."

"Oh, that's right," Scott realized. "Well, Dandy is a good pleasure horse. I just can't get him to lope on the correct lead."

"Leads are important in pleasure classes," Garnet had to agree. Then she sighed. "Scott, I wish I could help you. Since I can't, would you please lead me around again on Sparkler?"

"That's what I came for," he said.

With Scott at Sparkler's head, Garnet checked the girth nervously. She hoped she could find the courage to get on the horse again. With one big effort, she forced herself to get up quickly. She gained courage from Sparkler's steadiness. They walked around the pasture for some time. Garnet would signal with her leg and then her voice. If the horse did not obey then Scott would direct him.

When they had finished, Garnet couldn't thank Scott enough. What a good friend he was. And she was so terribly proud of Sparkler.

Scott agreed that the horse learned quickly. "That horse knows almost as much as Dandy and I do already. I wish the fair had a class that we could win. I'd like a class where you only have to know how to walk, stop, and turn."

Garnet stared at him. "Scott, that's it! There is a class like that. It's called the Trail class. You could get a ribbon in that with a little coaching."

Scott looked doubtful. "Trail class? What do I have to do? I've never even seen one."

With excitement, she told him all about it. There would be objects for the horses to walk by or carry. They would have to cross a bridge or cavalletti. Some obstacles would call for backing or sidepassing. Usually everything was done at the walk so leads were not important.

"What's cavalletti? What's sidepassing?" he asked.

"Cavelletti," Garnet explained, "is just a fancy name for a few logs laid parallel to each other. The horse should pick up his feet as he goes over them. Sidepassing means the horse moves sideways without turning his body."

Scott began to get excited, too. "Gee, that does sound like a neat class. Are there many people in it?"

"No," she told him eagerly. "That's the best part. Most people are afraid of the unknown. And working individually gives them stage fright."

"Do you think Dandy could learn all that stuff in time?" Scott asked.

"Sure he could. I've seen lots of Trail classes. I could help you," she offered.

"Great! Can we start this afternoon? Come over to my house and we'll set up some stuff to practice on."

"All right," Garnet agreed.

Then Scott had an idea. "Garnet," he urged. "Why don't you enter Sparkler in that class, too? He would go anywhere for you."

"But Sparkler is just a baby," she protested. "He hasn't done anything but walk so far."

"So?" Scott continued eagerly. "He trusts you. You can teach him the rest by fair time. Come on, we'll do it together."

Garnet didn't know what to say. She didn't think the Trail class would hurt Sparkler. He wouldn't have to canter or anything. It was a tempting idea. If Mrs. Grant saw Garnet riding Sparkler in the fair show, Jeff Pierce would never get to train him. Maybe . . . .

"All right," Garnet decided. "We'll work on both horses. You can come over here mornings. I'll go over to your house in the afternoons."

"Terrific!" Scott cheered. "This will be fun."

"I hope so," she said. "Just don't get mad if I decide not to enter Sparkler after all. I don't want him hurt."

"Of course," Scott agreed. "Just wait until you

see how much he wants to please you. You'll want to enter him for sure then."

Garnet read up on sidepassing before she went to Scott's house. One of the books told all about how to teach it.

> Stand next to the horse, holding him still with one hand on the reins. The trainer should poke the horse with his thumb a little behind where the rider's leg would hang. When the horse moves sideways a few steps, reward him. Add a few more steps each day.

She knew this information might be a real advantage to them. Very few of the 4-H kids she knew had their horses trained to sidepass.

At Scott's they worked Dandy on the cavalletti first. Garnet showed Scott how a little extra squeeze with his legs would make Dandy pick up his feet. Soon the horse was missing all the logs every time.

She had Scott practice taking things out of a mailbox and putting on a raincoat while mounted. He tried carrying a noisy bunch of tin cans and a large tree branch on Dandy. They experimented with riding through a gate. Then they finished with a few steps of sidepassing from the ground. So far their plan seemed to be going well.

The next morning they repeated the lesson with Sparkler. The Arabian caught on even more quickly than Dandy had. But he got upset more easily, too.

After a week's work, Garnet began to think she really should enter Sparkler. Scott agreed. She would need her mom's signature for that. It was time to tell her mom her secret.

Garnet decided that Saturday would be the best time to surprise her mother. Her mom had the day off, and Jeannie had plans to go shopping.

Mrs. Grant was frosting a cake when Garnet said casually, "Mom, I have something to show you."

Her mother was half-listening. "Like what?" she asked.

"Oh, just something," Garnet said, smiling mysteriously. "All you have to do is look out the window in five minutes.

Mrs. Grant looked up. Now she was listening. "All right," she agreed. "I'll be looking."

Garnet raced off. She had Sparkler saddled and tied behind the barn. She slipped off the halter and swung up. She rode around the corner of the barn.

She could see her mom's face at the window. Now the face was pressed against the window. Then the back door flew open. Sparkler snapped to attention.

"It's all right," Garnet told him. "Everything's all right now."

Her mother came up and gave her daughter's hand a great big squeeze. "Oh, honey, this is wonderful," she said with tears in her eyes. "How did you ever manage this?"

"I had a little help from Scott Morgan," Garnet

admitted. "I just had to ride Sparkler so you wouldn't send him to Jeff Pierce."

Mrs. Grant smiled through her tears. "All right, you win. You are the only trainer this horse needs."

Garnet explained that she wanted to enter her horse in the fair. Her mom was doubtful. But when Garnet showed her what Sparkler could do she quickly agreed to give Garnet permission.

Nine

THE fairgrounds were just waking up. It was show day, and Garnet had been awake most of the night. It didn't seem possible that she was standing here, grooming her two-year-old Arabian for his first show. She was probably crazy to try such a thing. If only she could get it over with quickly!

"Today is the day," she told Sparkler. "I hope you aren't as nervous as I am."

Garnet knew she couldn't keep brushing until it was time for their class. The Trail class was always the last class of the show. Maybe she could help Scott get ready for his other classes.

She had to pass Jeannie's stall to get to Scott's. There was Jeannie, brushing the last imaginary dirt from Princess's coat. The palomino looked gorgeous. Something in Garnet made her hope Jeannie wouldn't win this time.

Almost at once Garnet felt guilty. How can I feel that way about my own sister? she wondered. Jeannie had worked hard. She deserved to win lots of classes *and* the Horseman of the Year award.

"Hi, Jeannie," Garnet began. "Princess looks beautiful. Anything I can do to help?"

Jeannie turned to her. "Oh, Garnet," she said sweetly. "No, thank you. I already have help."

Sure enough, a head popped up from behind Princess. Garnet was shocked. It was Scott. He had been down on his knees working on Jeannie's horse. Well, if he has time to help my sister, he certainly doesn't need my help, Garnet thought.

Without a word, Garnet disappeared into the crowd. She tried to concentrate on the show, but she was too angry. She could hardly clap when Jeannie took top honors in the Senior Showmanship class.

The games on horseback almost made Garnet forget to be angry. Then the riders in the Senior Western Pleasure class began to gather at the entry gate. She saw Jeannie leaning down from her palomino to talk to someone in a big cowboy hat. Is it Scott? she wondered.

The entry gate opened. The person wearing the cowboy hat handed his hat to Jeannie. She gave him a quick hug. It wasn't Scott. It was Jeff Pierce. No wonder Jeannie had been so eager to have Jeff train Sparkler.

Scott was already in the ring on Dandy. Garnet wondered if he had seen Jeannie and Jeff together. No, Scott had been ahead of them in line. If he only knew what a little sneak Jeannie was, he'd drop her for sure. But if he is that blind he deserves her, Garnet thought. She decided she wouldn't tell him.

She couldn't stand to watch the rest of the class. She went back to Sparkler's stall. At least Sparkler liked her better than Jeannie. She decided to get Sparkler ready a little early and take him for a walk.

The Arabian tried to nuzzle her as she saddled him. She laughed and patted his neck. He was so delighted to get out of the stall that he pranced along beside her. Then he spotted an extra-choice patch of grass and went over to it. He seemed so happy that she soon forgot all about the show.

Suddenly she heard someone call, "Garnet, hurry! Your class is next!" It was her mother.

Garnet turned to Sparkler. She mounted shakily and went toward the ring. The little Arabian moved confidently under her.

Scott was already in the group waiting for instructions. He smiled at her. He seemed to be trying to tell her something. She looked away.

Then the judge began to explain the course to them. They were to go through a gate, cross a bridge, step over the cavalletti, and carry a bucket of small rocks. The sidepassing was to be done over a big U formed by several logs. The horse was expected to keep his front feet on one side and his back feet on the other side as he turned. The last thing was a jump about eighteen inches high.

The first rider's number was called. As he rode toward the gate, the other riders began to whisper. They sounded worried about the sidepassing. Several of them had no idea how to sidepass.

Garnet was more concerned about the jump. She was sure Sparkler would jump if she asked him to. But Doc Holmes had said no cantering or jumping this year. Would one little jump make that much difference? she wondered.

All at once Dandy was beside them. "Garnet," whispered Scott, "I've been trying to talk to you all day. Where have you been?"

"What do you care?" she shot back.

"I was afraid you might have gotten the wrong idea about Jeannie and me," he said.

Garnet looked at him curiously. "What do you mean, 'the wrong idea'?"

"I was afraid you'd think we'd gotten back together," he explained.

"Well, haven't you?" she demanded.

"No," Scott whispered so loud that some of the others looked at him. He went on more quietly. "I realized this morning that I'd forgotten Dandy's hoof black. Jeannie said I could use some of hers if I'd do Princess first. Then you came along."

Garnet's face broke into a great big smile. "Oh, Scott, I'm so glad you explained. I was so mad at you both."

Just then Scott's number was called. "Good luck," Garnet whispered. He smiled back and gave her the "thumb's up" sign.

She was happy to see Dandy manage the first four obstacles perfectly. The sidepassing was next. The pressure was on. No one had done it right yet.

Scott positioned Dandy carefully. The horse's front and back feet were both the same distance from the end of the first log. Things went very well until the sharpest part of the turn. Then Dandy didn't turn quite enough. He stepped back over the log with his front feet and finished the U on that side. Scott would lose some points. Still, it was better than anyone else had done.

The jump gave Scott and Dandy no problem. Everyone else had done it easily, too.

Scott looked pleased as he joined the riders who were finished. Garnet formed a circle with her fingers to show her approval. Scott grinned back.

Garnet's number was the last one called. She got Sparkler close enough to the gate to raise the latch easily. Smoothly he backed through it. She was able to latch the gate again without even leaning from the saddle. There was a small ripple of applause.

The bridge, the cavalletti, and the rocks were easy. Garnet was so proud of her horse that she wanted to burst.

She positioned Sparkler perfectly for the sidepassing. He stepped exactly where she told him. They finished the U without a false step. There was a hearty applause this time.

The jump was next. Garnet would win the class

if Sparkler took it. She turned him toward it. The crowd waited expectantly.

Then there was a buzzing in the stands. Garnet had ridden past the jump and directly to the line of those that had finished.

The judge looked puzzled. He wrote on his card and handed it to the ringmaster. Scott was signaling "well done."

Garnet felt a little sad. She wondered what her mother would say. Would Mom think that I had done the right thing? Mom seems to like winners, Garnet thought.

As Scott rode forward to accept his first place trophy, Garnet realized she was proud of her student. She was proud of Sparkler, too. The little two year old had done a remarkable job.

She was just leaving the ring when she heard the loudspeaker say, "Garnet Grant, will you please stay for a moment?" Have I done something wrong? she wondered.

The she saw Doc Holmes coming through the gate with a huge trophy. It was the Horseman of the Year award.

Doc motioned that she should come closer to the announcer's stand so that he could use the mike.

"Ladies and gentlemen," he began. "Every year several of us form a committee to award the Horseman of the Year trophy. We try to choose the 4-H rider who shows the greatest skill and concern for horses. This year's winner is a little unusual. She has not won a single class today. Instead, our winner gave a very nervous young horse enough confidence to complete the Trail class. Then she cared enough about the horse to purposely lose rather than take a jump she thought might harm him. Garnet Grant, I want to present the Horseman of the Year trophy to you with my congratulations."

Garnet was speechless. She slid off Sparkler in a flash. Such a small horse shouldn't have to carry such a large trophy. She started to cry. Everyone applauded.

Doc Holmes gave her a kiss on the cheek and

said, "Nice going, Rocky." Everyone stood up and cheered.

When it was all over, Garnet found her mom, Scott, and Jeannie jumping up and down with excitement.

"Oh, Garnet, that was wonderful," cried Mrs. Grant.

Jeannie gave her a big hug. "Garnet, I'm so proud of you," she said. "I guess I just didn't know a winner when I saw one."

GLOSSARY OF TERMS

Arabian: a breed of horse known for its graceful build, speed, intelligence and spirit

Canter: a controlled version of a horse's three-beat gait

Gelding: a male horse that cannot be a father

Girth: the strap that holds the saddle on

Halter: rope or strap for leading or tying

Lead: the set of legs that strike out the farthest at the canter; on a circle, a horse leads with the inside front leg

Lope: a very slow canter done by western horses

Lunge: a sudden forceful forward movement

Mare: a female horse that is four years or older

Palomino: a golden brown horse with white points (trim)

Pneumonia: a disease of the lungs caused by infection

Quarter Horse: a breed of short muscular horses developed by the cowboys

Ringworm: contagious disease caused by fungi with ring-shaped discolored patches on the skin

Stallion: male horse over the age of three

About the Author

MARILYN D. ANDERSON grew up on a dairy farm in Minnesota. Her love for animals and her twenty-plus years of training and showing horses are reflected in many of her books.

A former music teacher, Marilyn has taught band and choir for seventeen years. She specialized in percussion and violin. She stays busy training young horses, riding in dressage shows, working at a library, giving piano lessons, and, of course, writing books.

Marilyn and her husband live in Bedford, Indiana.

Other books by Marilyn D. Anderson include *The Horse That Came to Breakfast, I Don't Want a New Horse!* and *We Have to Get Rid of These Puppies!*